KNOT NOW!

The Complete Friendship Bracelet Kit!

CONTENTS

1. Use the strings on the front cover to make all of the fabulous friendship bracelets in this book.

2. Use the ruler printed on the back cover for measuring string.

3. To use the string, find the loose end and gently pull.

   Measure and cut off the string according to the instructions.

4. Before you begin, cut off a piece of string just long enough to go around your wrist. Keep this string to remind you how long your bracelets should be.

5. To hold your bracelet in place while you work on it, you can tape it to a table or desktop (be sure to ask a grown-up if it's OK), or clip it to a clipboard (but you'll need something to keep the clipboard in place).

6. Most bracelets begin and end with a knot. The best knot to use is an OVERHAND KNOT:

7. After you have finished your design, a nice way to close the bracelet is with a SQUARE KNOT:

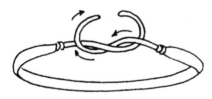 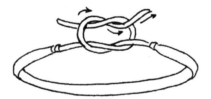 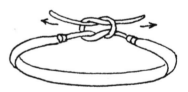

Put the right end over the left end, then under and back over again.

Now put that same end over the other end, then under and back over it.

Pull the ends tightly!

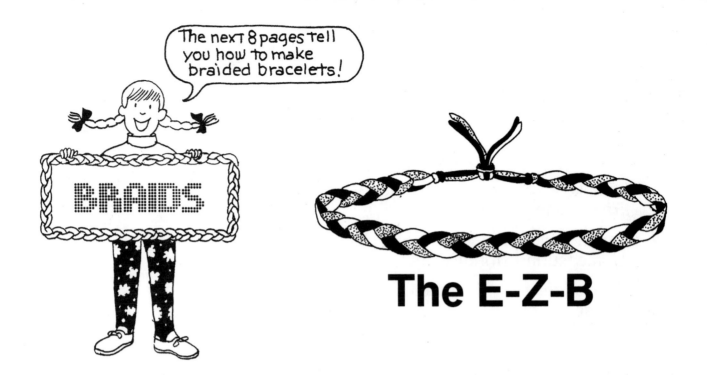

The E-Z-B

How to make the E-Z-B:

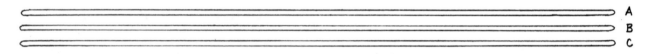

1. You will need three different colored strings (A,B,C), each 24 inches long.

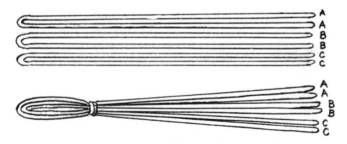

2. Fold the strings in half. Tie a knot near the top. Now you have six strings to work with.

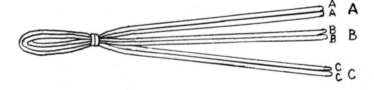

Note: Put the strings of the same color together to make three thicker strands (A,B,C).

3. Tape the loop to a tabletop. Now you are ready to braid!

 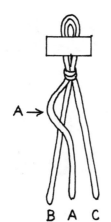 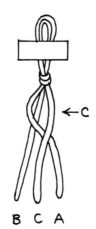 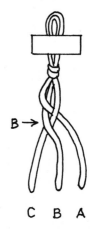

A B C — B A C — B C A — C B A

4. Arrange the colors like this: A,B,C.

Start on the left with A. Put A over B. (Now A is in the middle!)

Put C over A. (Now C is in the middle!)

Put B over C. (Now B is in the middle!)

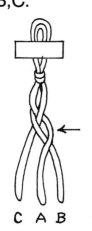 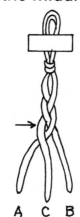 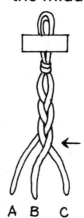 

C A B — A C B — A B C — B A C

Put A over B. — Put C over A. — Put B over C. — Keep braiding!

loop

loose ends

5. When the bracelet is long enough to go around your wrist, stop braiding. Tie the loose ends together with a knot.

6. To close the bracelet, wrap the loose ends once around the loop. Then put the ends through the loop as shown. Pull tightly to make a knot.

8-Looper

How to make the 8-Looper:

1. You will need one 48-inch string of one color (A), and two 12-inch strings of another color (B).

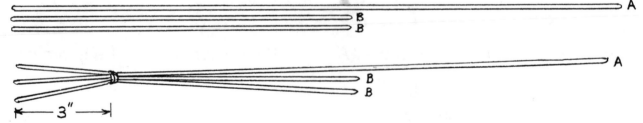

├─── 3" ───┤

2. Tie the three strings together with a knot 3 inches from the top.

Note: When you make the 8-Looper, you will be braiding with only the long string (A).

3. Tape the short ends of the strings
to a tabletop.

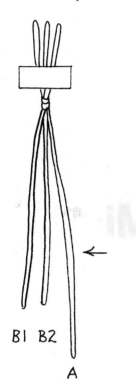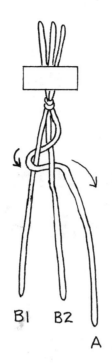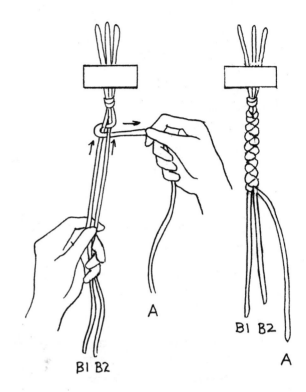

4. Arrange the colors
like this: B_1, B_2, A.

Put A over B_2 and then
under B_1, back over B_1,
and then under B_2.
You have just made
a figure-eight loop!

**Pull A so the loop slides all the
way up to the knot. Pull it very
tightly.** Keep making the same
figure-eight loops. After each
loop, pull A up tightly!

5. When the braid is long enough to go around your wrist,
stop braiding. Tie a knot where you stopped.

6. To close the bracelet, tie a square knot.
(See page 3 for directions.) Pull the ends tightly!

Jewel-in-the-Middle

How to make the Jewel-in-the-Middle:

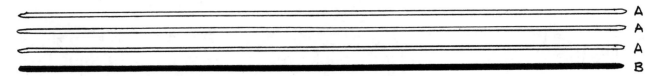

1. You will need three 30-inch strings of one color (A),
and one 30-inch string of another color (B).

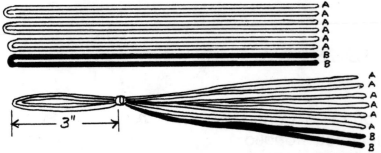

2. Fold the strings in half. Tie them together with a knot 3 inches
from the top. Now you have eight strings to work with.

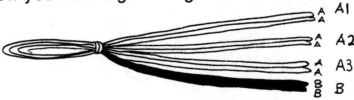

Note: Put two strings of the same color together
to make four thicker strands (A_1, A_2, A_3, B).

8

3. Tape the loop to a tabletop.

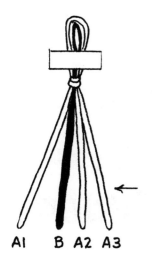

A1　B　A2　A3

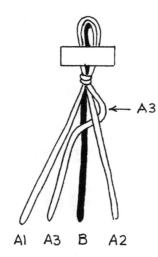

←—A3

A1　A3　B　A2

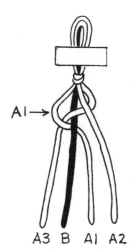

A1—→

A3　B　A1　A2

4. Arrange the colors like this: A_1, B, A_2, A_3. Start on the right with A_3.

Put A_3 under A_2 and then over B. Leave A_3 between B and A_1.

Put A_1 over A_3 and then under B. Leave A_1 between B and A_2.

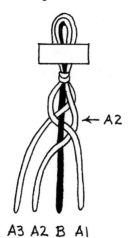

←—A2

A3　A2　B　A1

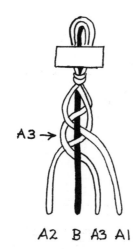

A3—→

A2　B　A3　A1

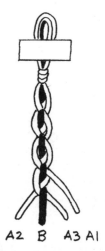

A2　B　A3　A1

Put A_2 under A_1, then over B. Leave A_2 between A_3 and B.

Put A_3 over A_2, then under B. Leave A_3 between B and A_1.

After each step, pull the strings up tightly!

5. Keep braiding until the bracelet is long enough to go around your wrist. Tie the loose ends together with a knot.

6. To close the bracelet, wrap the loose ends around the loop, then pull the ends through the loop as shown. Pull tightly.

Buddy Binder

How to make the Buddy Binder:

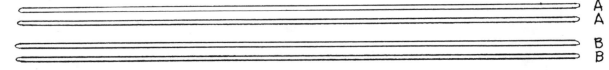

1. You will need two 30-inch strings of one color (A), and two 30-inch strings of another color (B).

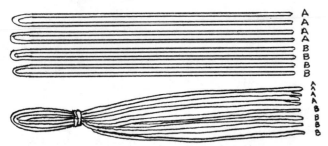

2. Fold the strings in half. Tie them together with a knot near the top. Now you have eight strings to work with.

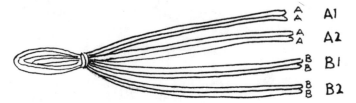

Note: Put two strings of the same color together to make four thicker strands (A_1, A_2, B_1, B_2).

3. Tape the loop to a tabletop.

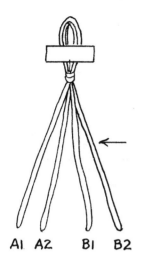

A1 A2 B1 B2

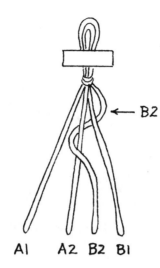

A1 A2 B2 B1

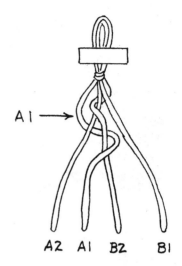

A2 A1 B2 B1

4. Arrange the colors like this: A_1, A_2, B_1, B_2. Start on the right with B_2.

Put B_2 under B_1 and under A_2, then bring back over A_2. Leave B_2 between A_2 and B_1.

Now take A_1 on the left. Put A_1 under A_2 and under B_2, then back over B_2. Leave A_1 between A_2 and B_2.

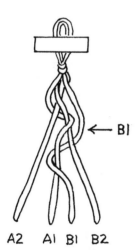

A2 A1 B1 B2

Now take B_1 and put it under B_2 and under A_1, then back over A_1. Leave B_1 between A_1 and B_2.

5. Tie the ends together with a knot.

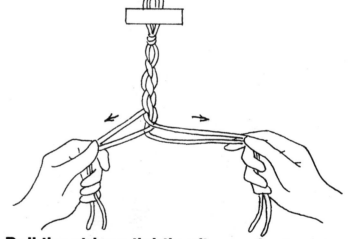

Pull the strings tightly after each step.
Keep braiding until the bracelet is long enough to go around your wrist.

6. To close the bracelet, wrap the ends around the loop. Pull the ends through the loop as shown. Pull tightly.

Twin Twisters are twice as nice 'cause they're so easy to do!

Twin Twister

How to make the Twin Twister:

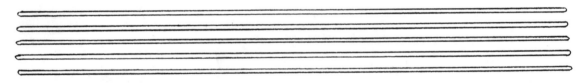

1. You will need five different colored strings, each 24 inches long.

|← 3" →|

2. Tie the strings together with a knot 3 inches from the top.

3. Tape the short ends of the strings to a tabletop.

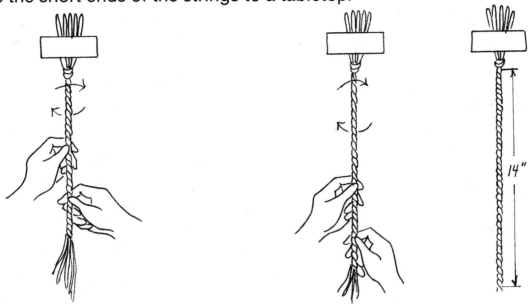

4. Hold the strings together as a group and twist them. Keep twisting in the same direction.

Twist tightly, making the twist longer as you go. Make a very tight twist about 14 inches long.

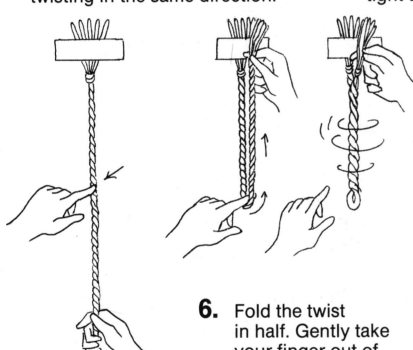

5. Hold the twist with one hand. Put a finger from your other hand in the middle of the twist. Press down.

6. Fold the twist in half. Gently take your finger out of the middle of the twist—the twist will twist around itself! (Don't worry if the twist bunches up. You can smooth it out.) Untape the twist from the table.

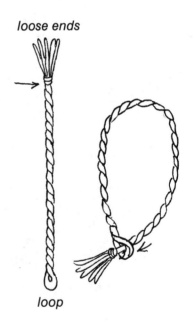

loose ends

loop

7. Tie the loose ends together with a knot. To close the bracelet, pull the knotted end through the loop on the other end as shown.

Big Band

How to make the Big Band:

1. You will need five different colored strings (A,B,C,D,E), each 30 inches long.

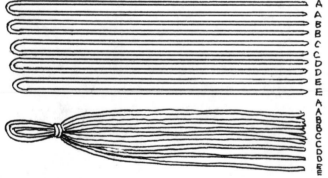

2. Fold the strings in half. Tie them together with a knot near the top. Now you have ten strings to work with.

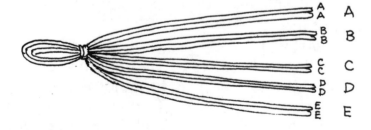

Note: Put the strings of the same color together to make five thicker strands (A,B,C,D,E).

3. Tape the loop to a tabletop. **When making the Big Band, always weave with the strand on the right!**

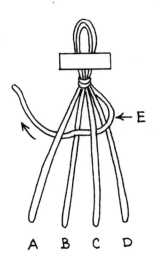

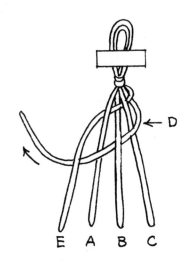

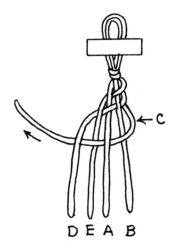

4. Arrange the strings like this: A,B,C,D,E. Start on the right with E. Put E over D, under C, over B, and under A. Pull E up tightly. Leave E on the left.

Now take D and put it over C, under B, over A, and under E. Pull D up tightly. Leave D on the left.

Now take C and put it over B, under A, over E, and under D. Pull C up tightly. Leave C on the left.

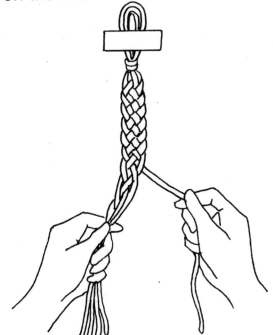

5. Hold on firmly to the strings as you weave. Keep weaving until the bracelet is long enough to go around your wrist.

6. Tie the loose ends together with a knot. To close the bracelet, wrap the ends around the loop. Pull the ends through the loop as shown. Pull tightly.

It's called toe weaving but you do it with your fingers!

Toe Weaving

How to do Toe Weaving:

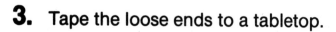

1. You will need three different colored strings, each 30 inches long.

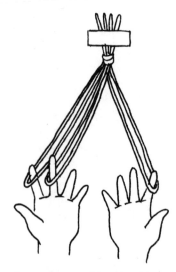

2. Fold the strings in half.

Tie the strings together with a knot about 5 inches from the loose ends, so you have three very long loops.

3. Tape the loose ends to a tabletop.

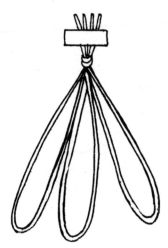

4. Separate the loops like this.

Hold your hands with the palms up, facing you. **Always keep your palms up as you work.**

Put your fingers in the loops like this. Now you are ready to begin weaving.

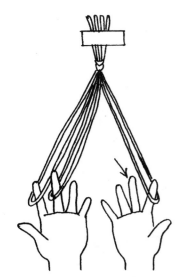
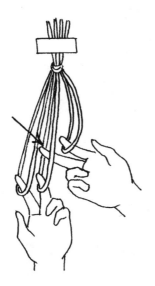
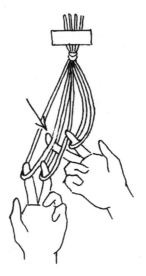
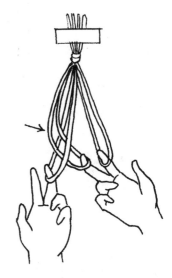

5. Use your right middle finger to hook with. **Always hook with the middle fingers.**

Put your right middle finger up through the first loop as shown.

Hook the second loop with the tip of your right middle finger.

Pull the second loop off your left index finger and back through the first loop.

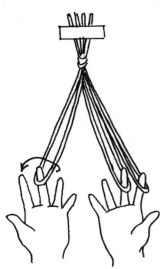
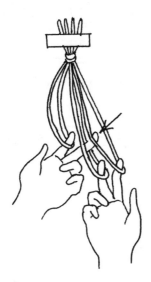
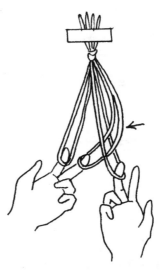
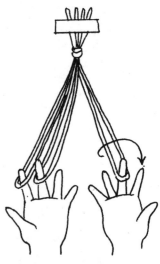

Now the loops on your fingers will look like this. Slip the loop on your left middle finger onto your left index finger.

Now hook with your left middle finger. Put the finger up through the first loop and hook the second loop with your fingertip.

Pull the loop off your right index finger and back through the first loop. **After each stitch, pull your hands apart to make it tight.**

Now the loops will look like this. **Always move the loop on your middle finger over to your empty index finger.**

6. Keep on weaving until the bracelet is long enough to go around your wrist. Tie a knot. To close the bracelet, wrap the loose ends around the loop. Pull the ends through the loop as shown. Pull tightly.

The next 6 pages are all about bracelets with knots!

Spinning Spiral

How to make the Spinning Spiral:

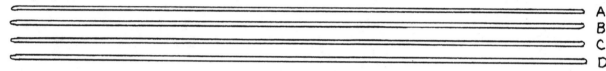

A
B
C
D

1. You will need four different colored strings (A,B,C,D), each 30 inches long.

A
B
C
D

|← 5" →|

2. Tie the strings together with a knot about 5 inches from the top.

Note: One basic knot is used in all the knotted bracelets. Here's how to do it:

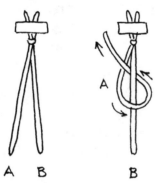

Put A over B, then back under B and over A.

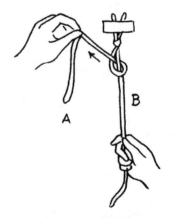

Hold B firmly as you pull A up tightly.

3. To begin, tape the short ends of the strings to a tabletop.
When you make the Spinning Spiral, always knot from the left!

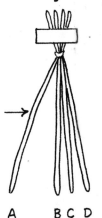

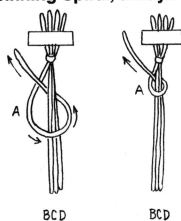

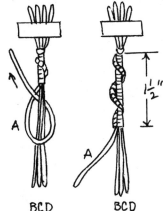

A   B C D   BCD   BCD   BCD   BCD

4. Arrange the colors like this: A,B,C,D. Start with string A on the left. Hold B, C, and D together like one string (BCD).

Make the basic knot with A: Put A over the other three strings (BCD), then under them and back over A. Hold BCD firmly as you pull A up tightly.

Keep knotting with A for about 1½ inches. **Keep the knots close together and pull A up tightly after each knot.**

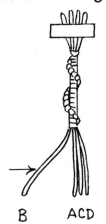

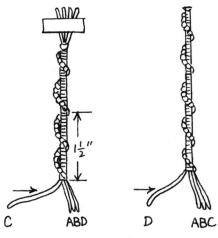

B   ACD   ACD   C   ABD   D   ABC

5. Now start knotting with a new color, B. Hold A, C, and D together like one string (ACD).

Make the basic knot with B: Put B over the other three strings (ACD), then under them and back over B. Pull B up tightly after each knot. Do this for 1½ inches.

Now knot with C around strings ABD for 1½ inches. Then knot with D around ABC.

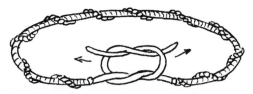

6. After knotting with D for 1½ inches, stop knotting and tie all the ends together with a knot.

7. To close the bracelet, tie the ends together with a square knot. (See page 3 for directions.)

Candy Stripe

How to make the Candy Stripe:

1. You will need four different colored strings (A,B,C,D), each 36 inches long.

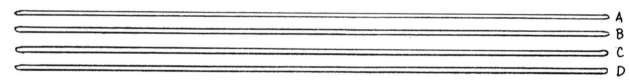

2. Tie the strings together with a knot about 3 inches from the top.

Note: The Candy Stripe is made with just one basic double knot. It takes 5 inches of string to make 1 inch of knots! That's why you need such long strings. To make a wider bracelet, just use more strings! (But they will have to be even longer.)

3. Tape the short ends of the strings to a tabletop.
Remember to always knot from the left.

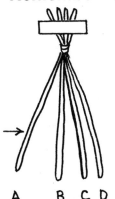 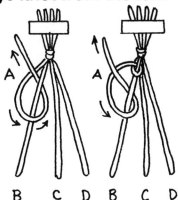 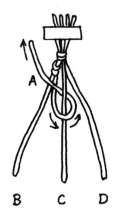 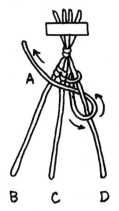

| A | B C D | B C D B C D | B C D | B C D |

4. Arrange the colors like this: A,B,C,D. Start on the left with A.

Put A over B, then under B and back over A. Hold B firmly as you pull A up tightly. Make a second knot with A the same way. Pull it tightly.

Now put A over C, then under C and back over A. Pull up tightly. Make a second knot the same way. Pull tightly.

Put A over D, then under D and over A. Pull up tightly. Make a second knot. Now the first row is done.

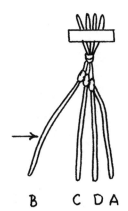 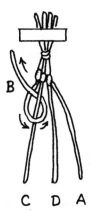 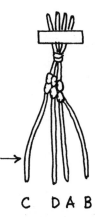 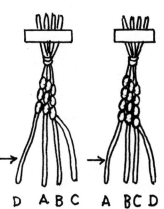

| B C D A | C D A | C D A B | D A B C   A B C D |

5. To start the next row, go back to the left and knot with B.

With B, tie double knots around C, then D, then A. After each knot pull B up tightly.

For the next row, go back to the left and knot with C. Tie double knots around D, then A, then B. Pull tightly.

Keep knotting row by row. **Remember to hold the strings firmly and pull the knots tightly!**

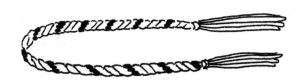 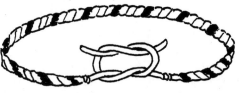

6. Keep knotting until the bracelet is long enough to go around your wrist. Tie a knot at the end.

7. To close the bracelet, tie a square knot. (See page 3 for directions.)

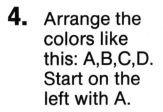

21

Sharp Chevron

(Try doing the Candy Stripe first to get ready for this one.)

How to make the Sharp Chevron:

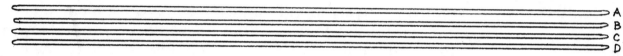

1. You will need four different colored strings (A,B,C,D), each 2 yards long.

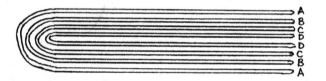

2. Fold the strings in half.

Tie the strings together near the top. Now you have eight strings to work with.

Note: The Sharp Chevron is the hardest bracelet in the book—because you have to knot from the LEFT and from the RIGHT, like this:

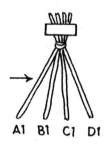

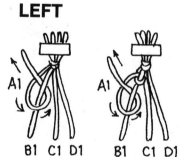

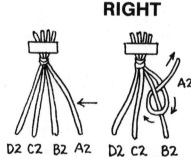

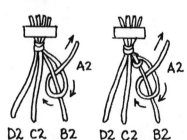

LEFT	**RIGHT**

Start on the left with A_1.

Put A_1 over B_1, then under B_1 and back over A_1. Hold B_1 firmly and pull A_1 tightly. Repeat the knot.

Start on the right with A_2.

Put A_2 over B_2, then under B_2 and back over A_2. Hold B_2 firmly and pull A_2 tightly. Repeat the knot.

3. To begin, tape the loop to a tabletop.

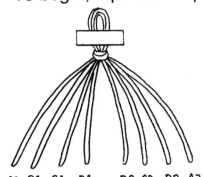

A1 B1 C1 D1   D2 C2 B2 A2

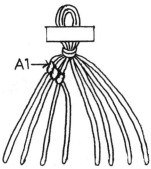

A1→   B1 C1 D1 A1   D2 C2 B2 A2

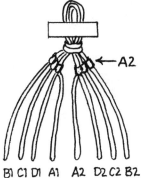

←A2   B1 C1 D1 A1   A2 D2 C2 B2

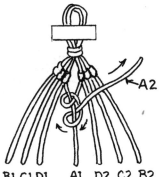

↗ A2   ←A2   B1 C1 D1   A1 D2 C2 B2

4. Arrange the strings like this. For strings A₁,B₁,C₁, and D₁ make the basic double knots from the LEFT. For A₂,B₂,C₂, and D₂ make the double knots from the RIGHT. **(See Note.)**

Begin knotting from the LEFT with A₁. Make double knots with A₁ around B₁, then C₁, then D₁. **Leave A₁ between D₁ and D₂.**

Now go to A₂ and knot from the RIGHT. Make double knots with A₂ around B₂, then C₂, then D₂.

Now make a double knot with A₂ around A₁. (You are still knotting from the RIGHT.) Now the first row is done!

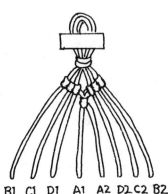

B1 C1 D1 A1   A2 D2 C2 B2

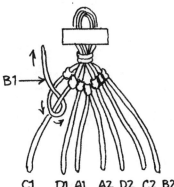

B1→   C1   D1 A1   A2 D2 C2 B2

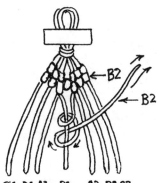

←B2   ←B2   C1 D1 A1 B1   A2 D2 C2

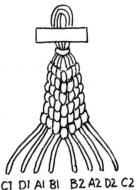

C1 D1 A1 B1   B2 A2 D2 C2

5. Your strings should now look like this, with A₁ and A₂ in the middle. Now you're ready to do the second row.

Start the second row on the LEFT with B₁. Make double knots with B₁ around C₁, then D₁, then A₁. **Leave B₁ between A₁ and A₂.**

Now go to the RIGHT and knot with B₂. Make double knots with B₂ around C₂, then D₂, then A₂, then B₁. The second row is done!

Knot row by row from the outsides to the middle until the bracelet is long enough to go around your wrist. **Don't forget to knot the two strings in the middle!**

6. Tie the loose ends together with a knot. To close the bracelet, wrap the loose ends around the loop, then pull them back through the loop as shown. Pull tightly.

MORE HINTS

1. Experiment with the bracelet designs! Try different color combinations, or arrange the colors in a different order. You'll be surprised how changing colors will change the design.

2. Try combining patterns. For instance, braid the ends of a knotted design. Or try inventing your own designs and patterns.

3. To make thinner braided or woven bracelets, use single strands of each color. Or make them thicker with several strings of each color held together and used as one strand of that color.

4. To make the "Candy Stripe" or the "Sharp Chevron" wider, use more strings—but be sure to work each string separately. (Remember, the wider your bracelet is, the longer the strings will have to be.)

5. Make friendship bracelets for your friends and family as gifts. Make pink, red, and white ones for Valentine's Day, red and green ones for Christmas, blue and white ones for Hanukkah, and orange and black ones for Halloween.

6. If you need more string, check your local dime store or craft store. Look for "embroidery floss"—it makes the best bracelet string!

HAVE KNOTS OF FUN!